snake cake

Yukiko Kido

flip-a
WORD

Blue Apple

Word Families

The world is full of print. Written words are everywhere. It's impossible to learn printed words by memorizing them word, by word, by word. To make learning easier, words can be grouped into families.

The words in a word family have two or more letters that are the same. We read "at" words and "op" words, "it" words and "ug" words. If you know "at," then it's easier to learn bat, hat, and rat.

This book has words from three different word families. All the words in a family rhyme—which means you can add other words to the group by changing the first letter.

It's okay if some of the words you think of are not *real* words. If you make "dat" or "wat" or "lat," it's not wrong— as long as you know the difference between a real word and a nonsense word.

Flip each page and presto-change-o— a new word appears!

The

ake

Family

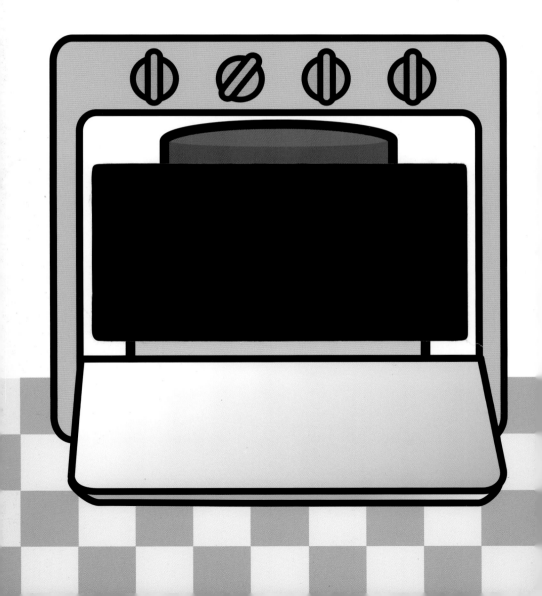

rake

snake bakes

snake on a rake

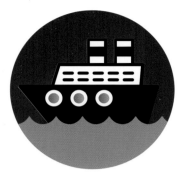

The oat Family

f
l
w
m
g
n
b
r
d
w
t

float

b o a t

goat floats

goat in a coat

goat floats on a boat

The ant Family

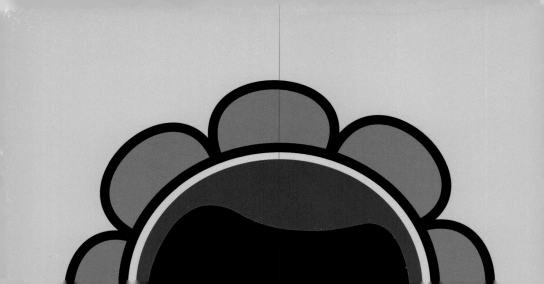

slant

ant on plant

pants on ant

plant on a slant

The ake Family

snake	fake
cake	take
bake	lake
rake	wake

The oat Family

boat	oat
float	moat
goat	throat
coat	bloat

The ant Family

ant	plant
pants	chant
slant	rant

Find the words in each family.